I'm Reading About

IOWA

The Hawkeye State!

GALLOPADE

by Carole Marsh

Printed and Manufactured in Peachtree City, GA., USA
www.gallopade.com

Book design: John Hanson

Editorial manager: Janice Baker

Iowa is a great state.

It is one of a kind.

What makes Iowa special?

Let's read about it

and see!

NATIVE AMERICANS

Who lived in Iowa first?

Native Americans did!

They moved around to find food.
They hunted in Iowa's woods.
They fished in Iowa's rivers.
They gathered fruits and seeds and nuts.

EXPLORERS

The first explorers came to Iowa in 1673.
They traveled down the Mississippi River.
Their names were Father Jacques Marquette
and Louis Joliet.
They came from France.

SETTLEMENT

A man named Julien Dubuque came to Iowa.
He was a fur trader.
He settled near the Mississippi River.
The city of Dubuque is named after him!

Iowa is the only state name that begins with two vowels.

Dubuque

STATEHOOD

Iowa was the 29th state to join the United States of America!

Isn't it great,
to be a state!
I bet Iowa
could hardly wait!

Iowa became a state in 1846.

Iowa
The 29th
State
Here we are!

FLAG

I am the state flag.
I was adopted in 1921.

What colors am I?
Blue. White. Red.

Look at me.
What else do you see?

I fly high over the state of Iowa!

OUR LIBERTIES WE PRIZE AND OUR RIGHTS WE WILL MAINTAIN
IOWA

CAPITAL

Say hello to Des Moines,
the capital city of Iowa!

There is an important building in Des Moines.
It is the State Capitol.
Iowa's laws are made there!

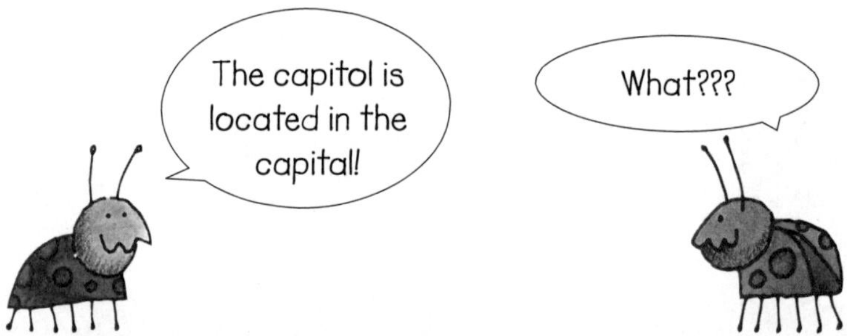

Capitol

SEAL

I am a seal,
but I am not the State Seal.
If I were, I would be very important.
I would be stamped on many official papers.
(Ouch, that might hurt!)

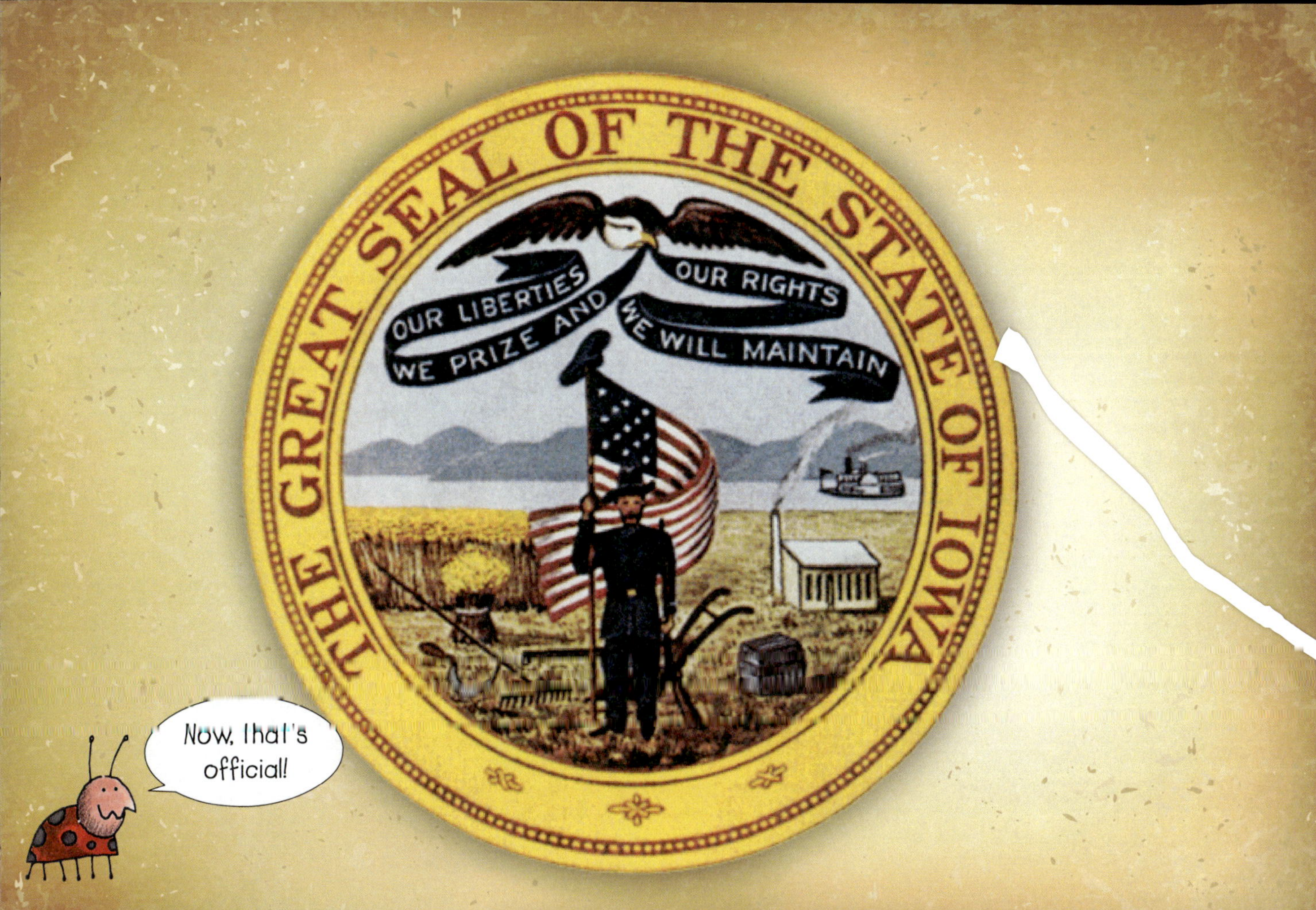
THE GREAT SEAL OF THE STATE OF IOWA
OUR LIBERTIES WE PRIZE AND
OUR RIGHTS WE WILL MAINTAIN
Now, that's official!

NICKNAME

State nicknames are fun!
State nicknames are great!
They share fun facts
about each state!

Iowa's nickname is "The Hawkeye State."

The word "Hawkeye" is in honor of Indian Chief Black Hawk.

The Hawkeye State

BORDERS

Look at Iowa.
Iowa is in a region called "the Midwest."

Iowa borders six other states.
Find them on the map!

Borders

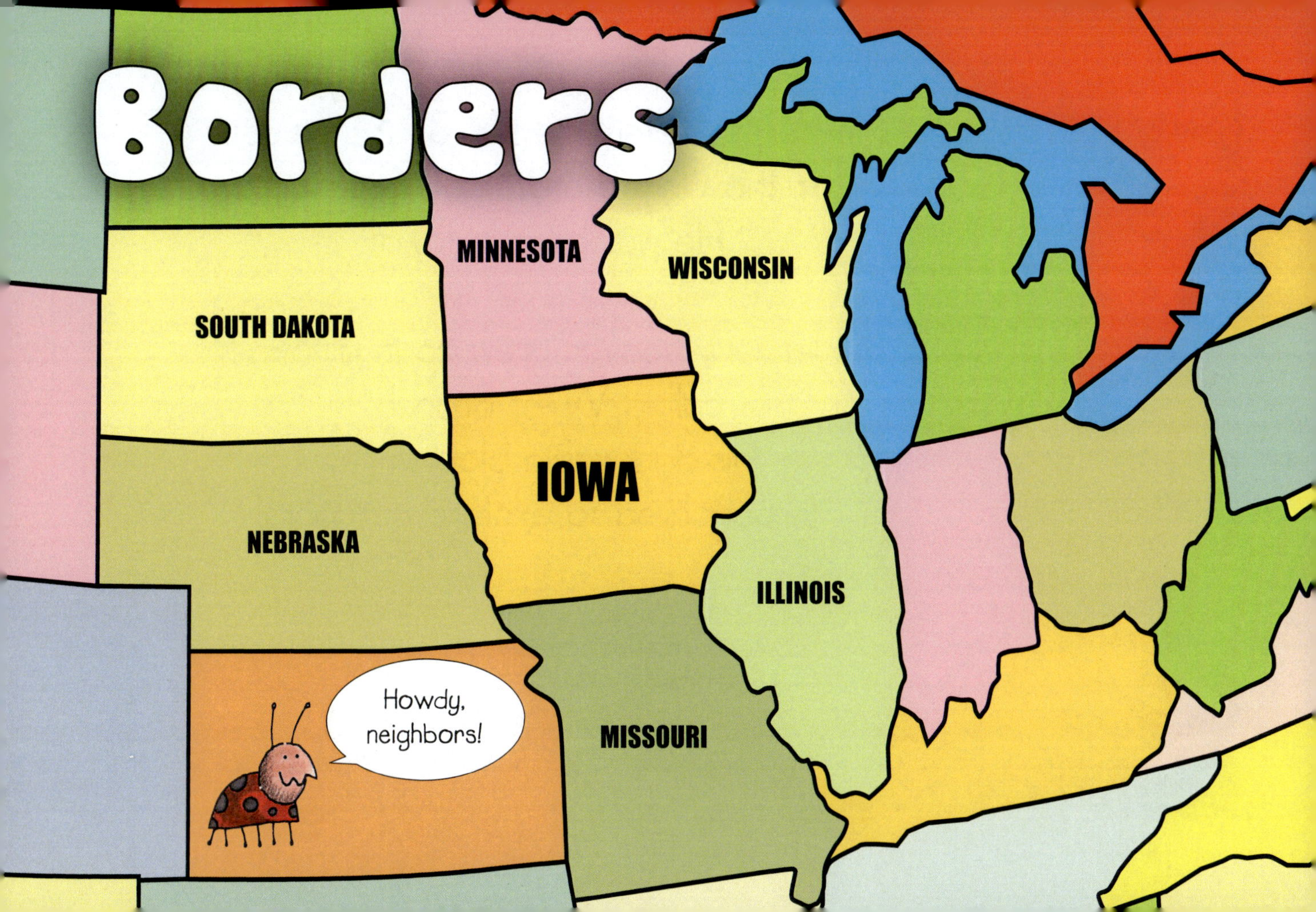
MINNESOTA
WISCONSIN
SOUTH DAKOTA
IOWA
NEBRASKA
ILLINOIS
MISSOURI
Howdy, neighbors!

PRESIDENT

Herbert Hoover was the 31st President of the United States of America. He was born in Iowa!

Herbert Hoover grew up in a town called West Branch. His dad was a blacksmith. Herbert liked to explore outdoors!

Herbert Hoover

PEOPLE

Many famous people

William "Buffalo Bill" Cody

Soldier, buffalo hunter, and famous showman

Carrie Chapman Catt

Worked to get women the right to vote

Grant Wood

Artist best known for his painting called *American Gothic*

call our state home!

George Gallup

Creator of the Gallup poll to measure people's opinions

Glenn Miller

Musician who led one of the best-known big bands

Shawn Johnson

Gymnast who won a gold medal at the 2008 Olympics

Eastern Goldfinch

I am the state bird, and I fly
over Iowa, proud and high.

As I fly, up in the sky,
I flap my wings to tell you "Hi!"

The Iowa state bird is the Eastern Goldfinch.

BIRD

Wild Rose

FLOWER

I am the Wild Rose.
I am the state flower.

I grow where it's warm and sunny.
I bloom in spring and summer.
I help make Iowa beautiful!

Look at me! Smell me!
My fruit can be cooked
to make a sweet jelly!

Oak

TREE

I am an Oak—I'm the state tree.
All over Iowa is where to find me.

My roots run deep, they keep me strong.
I can live for hundreds of years—that's very long!

I stand up straight, big and tall.
Don't climb too high—it would hurt to fall!

Geode

ROCK

I am a geode.
I am the state rock.

On the outside, I look like a rock.
But crack me open, and you will be amazed!
I have beautiful crystals inside!

Many geodes have been found in Iowa.
The town of Keokuk is known as the "Geode Capital of the World"!

Rivers

RIVERS

Iowa has many rivers.
People like to use them for boating and fishing!

Rivers were Iowa's first highways.
People floated down the rivers
on flatboats.
They carried goods
to sell or trade!

The river habitat is home to many animals:

Birds **Deer** **Snakes** **Frogs** **Fish** **and More!**

Iowa soil

SOIL

Iowa has an important natural resource.
It is Iowa's soil!

Plants grow very well in Iowa's soil.
That's why Iowa has so many farms.

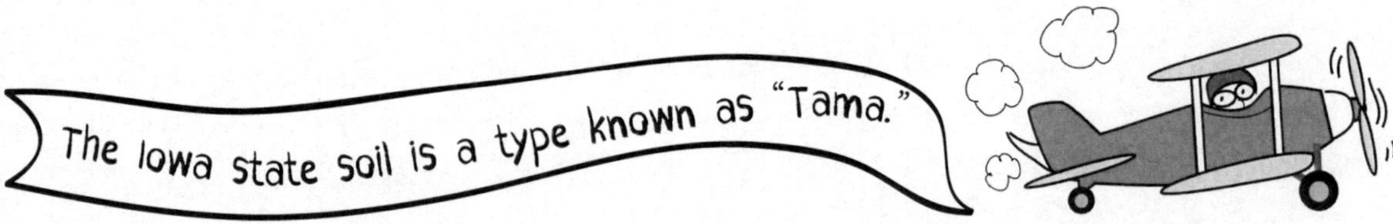

Loess Hills

Loess Hills

There are hills in western Iowa.
They are called the "Loess Hills."
Loose soil blown by the wind formed these hills.
It took many, many years to do it.

This habitat is home to many animals:

Deer Foxes Turtles Birds Butterflies and More!

Loess comes from a German word that means "loose."

Field of Dreams

LANDMARK

There is a beautiful baseball field near Dyersville.
It was built on farmland.
The field was built for the movie *Field of Dreams*.

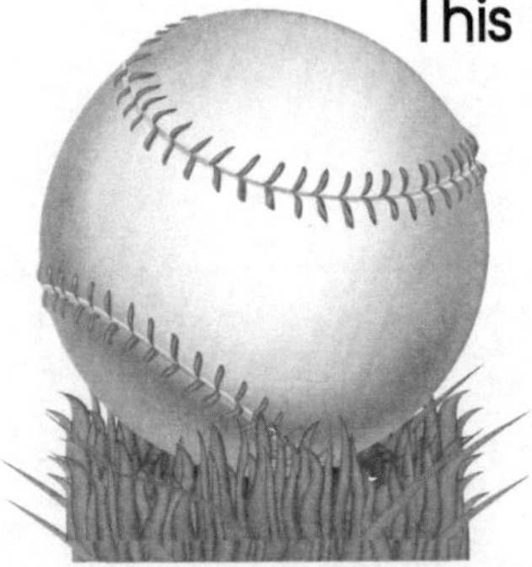

This baseball field is one of the most popular tourist attractions in Iowa.
Visitors can play ball on the field!

Iowa Crops

corn

Soybeans

oats and Hay

Apples

Apples are my personal favorite!

Iowa has many farms.
Why?
Because Iowa has good soil and a mild climate!

Some of the top crops grown in Iowa include:

Corn **Oats & Hay**
Soybeans **Apples**

Sports in Iowa

SPORTS

Baseball! Basketball! Football!
Iowa has it all.

Whether you like to watch or play,
You are sure to have a ball!

Hawkeyes **Cyclones** **Panthers**

Bulldogs

& More!

Iowa: Home of Corn

CLAIM TO FAME

When you think of Iowa, you think of corn!
Iowa is the #1 state for growing corn.

Corn is good food—for people and animals.
It is also used to make many products!

A typical ear of corn
has 800 kernels!

GLOSSARY

climate: weather conditions in an area over a long period of time

crystal: a clear, hard, shiny substance that has many sides

elect: to choose someone by voting

habitat: a place where plants or animals naturally live

laws: rules made by the government

natural resource: something found in nature that can be used by people

poll: an activity where people are asked questions to find out their opinions

region: an area that has similar characteristics

tourist: a person who visits a place for pleasure

typical: usual; normal